Dear Parent:
Your child's love of reading starts here!

Every child learns to read in a different way and at his or her own speed. Some go back and forth between reading levels and read favorite books again and again. Others read through each level in order. You can help your young reader improve and become more confident by encouraging his or her own interests and abilities. From books your child reads with you to the first books he or she reads alone, there are I Can Read Books for every stage of reading:

SHARED READING
Basic language, word repetition, and whimsical illustrations, ideal for sharing with your emergent reader

BEGINNING READING
Short sentences, familiar words, and simple concepts for children eager to read on their own

READING WITH HELP
Engaging stories, longer sentences, and language play for developing readers

READING ALONE
Complex plots, challenging vocabulary, and high-interest topics for the independent reader

ADVANCED READING
Short paragraphs, chapters, and exciting themes for the perfect bridge to chapter books

I Can Read Books have introduced children to the joy of reading since 1957. Featuring award-winning authors and illustrators and a fabulous cast of beloved characters, I Can Read Books set the standard for beginning readers.

A lifetime of discovery begins with the magical words "I Can Read!"

Visit www.icanread.com for information
on enriching your child's reading experience.

Bee Movie: The Honey Disaster Bee Movie ™ & © 2007 DreamWorks Animation L.L.C. All rights reserved. Printed in the United States of America. No part of this book may be used or reproduced in any manner whatsoever without written permission except in the case of brief quotations embodied in critical articles and reviews. For information address HarperCollins Children's Books, a division of HarperCollins Publishers, 1350 Avenue of the Americas, New York, NY 10019.
www.harpercollinschildrens.com

Library of Congress catalog card number: 2007932109
ISBN 978-0-06-125166-5
Book design by Rick Farley

First Edition

❖

DREAMWORKS

BEE MOVIE

The Honey Disaster

Adapted by Jennifer Frantz
Illustrations by Steven E. Gordon
and Kanila Tripp

HarperCollins*Publishers*

Barry Benson

could hardly believe his eyes.

But there it was,

jar after jar of honey.

"It's not 'right," Barry thought.

The humans were stealing honey!

Honey was made by bees for bees.

They worked hard to make honey.

Barry had to do something.

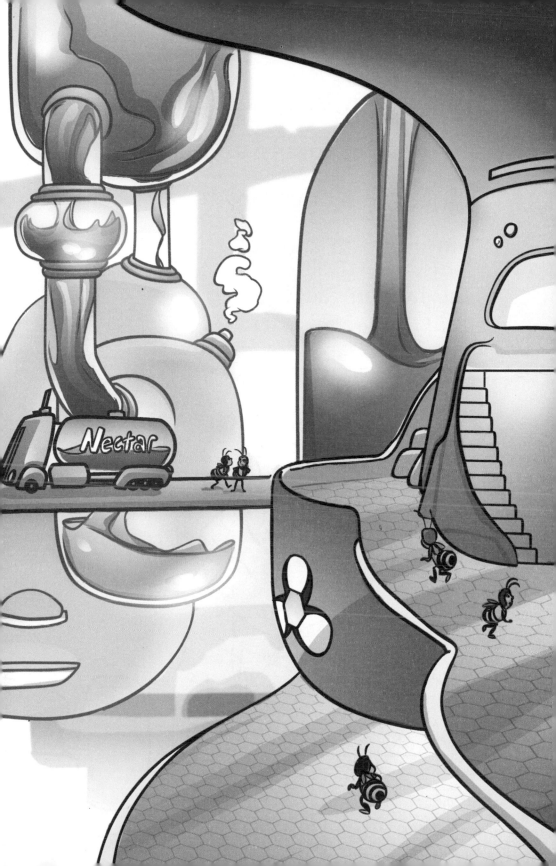

That night, Barry made a plan.
He told his family at dinner.
"I, Barry B. Benson,
am going to sue
the human race!"

On the day of the trial,
the courtroom was packed.
Barry's friends Adam and Vanessa
sat beside him.

Barry was first to speak
to the court.

"It's simple," he said.

"Bees make it, humans take it."

The trial went on. . . .

Barry said bees on honey farms

were treated badly.

Lawyers for the humans
fought back.

Finally, the judge
made up her mind.
"I agree with the bees," she said.

"We won!" Barry cried.

Humans had to give back
all of the honey.
It was collected
and returned to the bees.

Barry's plan was working.

The bees had never seen

so much honey!

Soon they had too much.

The bees stopped making honey.
Without work to fill their days,
the bees felt useless.

Even worse, all the flowers
began to die!

Flowers needed bees.

Bees spread pollen when

they gathered nectar for honey.

"Oh, no!" Barry cried.

His plan had gone wrong.

Barry had to fix things fast!

His friend Vanessa knew

all about flowers.

She could help.

Vanessa took Barry
to a big parade.
There were floats
full of fresh flowers just ahead.
Flowers are full of pollen!

Barry and Vanessa
snuck onto a float
and drove off!
They had to get the fresh flowers
home in a hurry.

When Barry and Vanessa got back,
the bees went to work.
They quickly spread pollen
from the fresh flowers.

In no time,

flowers were blooming.

Bees were buzzing.

And Barry B. Benson was busy
thinking about his next big adventure!